BIG CAT,
Little Kitty

To my new friend, J.X. —
Keep purring!
Susan Dill Detwiler

by Scotti Cohn
illustrated by Susan Detwiler

One fine Monday night, a big cat paces among the vines and trees. Her ears twitch and turn. She listens to every chirp, hoot, and screech.

"Who are you?" asks a gibbon. "And whose jungle is this?"

The big cat growls, "I am Tiger, and this is MY jungle."

She chases Gibbon up a tree.

That same night, a little kitty paces among the potted plants. Her ears twitch and turn. She listens to every chirp, buzz, and hum.

"Who are you?" asks a spider. "And whose porch is this?"

The little kitty growls, "I am Tiggy, and this is MY porch."

She chases Spider under a plant stand.

One Tuesday morning just after dawn, a big cat races across a vast plain. She runs so fast, she almost leaves her spots behind. When she is tired, she stretches out in the shade.

"Who are you?" asks a warthog. "And whose savannah is this?"

The big cat purrs, "I am Cheetah, and this is MY savannah."

Warthog decides he would feel safer in the big hole he made in the ground.

Very early that same morning, a little kitty races up and down the stairs. She runs so fast, her spots and stripes are a blur. When she is tired, she stretches out in front of a window.

"Who are you?" asks a mouse. "And whose house is this?"

The little kitty purrs. "I am Chessie, and this is MY house."

She jumps up. Mouse decides he would feel safer in his hole in the baseboard.

One Wednesday evening in the desert, a big cat stands on a rock and sniffs the air. His eyes blaze like the sun.

"Who are you?" asks a springbok. "And whose desert is this?"

The big cat's voice thunders in the dry wind. "I am Kalahari Lion, and this is MY desert."

Springbok scampers away.

That same evening in a garden, a little kitty sharpens his claws on a birch tree and sniffs the lilacs. His eyes are shiny like gold coins.

"Who are you?" asks a butterfly. "And whose garden is this?"

The little kitty puffs himself up. "I am Leonardo, and this is MY garden!"

Butterfly flitters away.

One Thursday afternoon, a big cat prowls through icy mountain shadows. Rose-shaped patterns curl through her thick smoky fur.

"Who are you?" asks a hare. "And whose mountain is this?"

The big cat leaps onto a frosty ledge. She hisses and yowls. "I am Snow Leopard, and this is MY mountain!"

Hare is lucky. He scoots into his burrow just in time.

That same afternoon, a little kitty wrapped in silvery fluff tiptoes across a frozen creek.

"Who are you?" asks a cardinal. "And whose park is this?"

The little kitty leaps onto a picnic table. She hisses and yowls. "I am Snowflake, and this is MY park!"

Cardinal is lucky. She only loses a few feathers.

One Friday, as the sun sinks behind the towering pines, a big cat stands on a rock. He waits and watches. His whiskers twitch.

"Who are you?" asks a bighorn sheep. "And whose forest is this?"

The big cat snarls. His eyes glitter like stars. "I am Cougar, and this is MY forest!"

Bighorn Sheep bounds up a hill to higher ground.

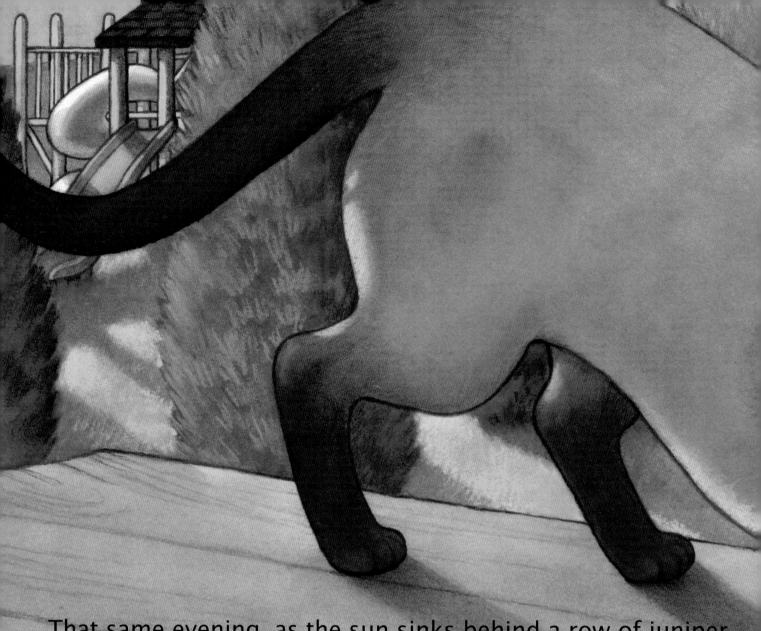

That same evening, as the sun sinks behind a row of juniper trees, a little kitty stands on a bench. He waits and watches. His whiskers twitch.

"Who are you?" asks a squirrel. "And whose playground is this?"

Little kitty crouches. His eyes glitter like stars. "I am Cato, and this is MY playground!"

Squirrel dashes up a tree and hides in the branches.

One fresh Saturday morning, a big cat paddles slowly across a lake. He climbs onto the shore.

"Who are you?" asks a young crocodile. "And whose lake is this?"

The big cat makes a deep coughing sound. "I am Jaguar, and this is MY lake."

He grabs Young Crocodile by the tail, but Young Crocodile wiggles free.

That same fresh morning, a little kitty prances by a pond. He stops and dips his paw into the water.

"Who are you?" asks a frog. "And whose pond is this?"

Little kitty pats the water with his paw. "I am Jingo, and this is MY pond!"

He wiggles his hips and pounces! Frog gets away. Little kitty gets wet.

One Sunday night, under a soft summer moon, a bobcat steps out of the woods. She smells fresh-cut grass. It feels prickly under her feet. She pauses and blinks.

Next to an evergreen hedge sits a little kitty. Beside her is a dog.

"Who are you?" asks Bobcat. "And whose backyard is this?"

Dog growls and barks. "I am King."

Little kitty hisses and puffs out her fur. "I am Queenie."

Together they shout, "This is OUR backyard!"

Just to scare them a little, Bobcat screams. Then she bounds across the lawn and disappears into the woods.

For Creative Minds

What Are Cats and How Are They Related?

Some people group all cats that roar and live in the wild (lions, tigers, jaguars, and leopards) as "big cats." Other people use the size and weight of the wild cats to group them, including the roaring cats, cougars, snow leopards, and cheetahs in the "big cat" group. Some people include bobcats, clouded leopards, lynx, and ocelots in the big cat group but other people put these cats in a "medium cat" group. Other people think of "big cats" as any wild cat, regardless of size. What do YOU think makes a cat a big cat?

Scientists all over the world use a scientific name for all living things. No matter where the scientists live or what language they speak, they all understand the scientific names. It also avoids confusion over phrases like "big cat." They sort or classify living things into groups, starting with very general sorts that get more and more specific: The two smallest (genus and species) groups become the scientific name.

> Cats are mammals (like us) in the Carnivora family—or meat-eating mammals.
> There are two major sub-families:

Cats that roar (Pantherinae)

lion:
Panthera leo

tiger:
Panthera tigris

jaguar:
Panthera onca

Cats that don't roar (Felinae)

bobcat:
Lynx rufus

cheetah:
Acinonyx jubatus

domestic (pet) cat:
Felis catus

snow leopard:
Uncia uncia

cougar:
Puma concolor

Cats of the World: A Map and Matching Activity

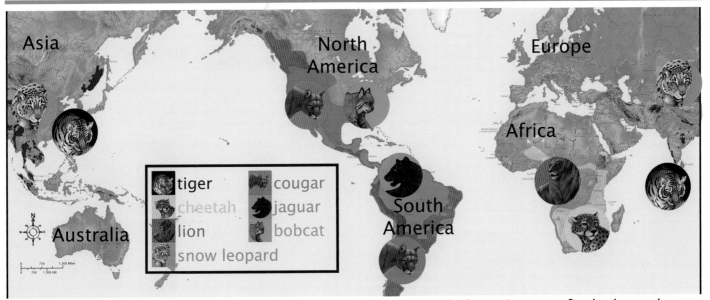

Match the cat to its description. Answers are upside down, below. Can you find where the cats live on the map?

 1 These endangered striped cats once roamed the jungles all across Asia but are now only found in isolated pockets.

 2 The world's fastest cats are found on Africa savannahs (grasslands) and a small section of Iran (in Asia). Their spots help them hide in the tall grass.

 3 Adult males are easily recognized by their manes. These great cats live in social groups called prides. They can be found in deserts, savannahs, and forests in parts of Africa and a small section of India.

 4 Living high in the snowy mountains of Central Asia, these endangered spotted cats are rarely seen by humans.

 5 This cat is known by many names including the one used in the book: mountain lion, panther, and puma. Solid in color, these cats can be found in many habitats in North, Central, and South America.

 6 All cats will swim if they have to but this particular type of cat likes swimming! Some are spotted and some are black but they all live in the Central and South American rainforests.

 7 Twice as big as an average domestic cat, these wild cats live in a wide range of habitats from southern Canada down to northern Mexico.

Answers: 1. Tigers; 2. Cheetahs; 3. Lions; 4. Snow Leopards; 5. Cougars (Mountain Lions, Pumas, or Panthers), 6. Jaguars; 7. Bobcats

Cat Senses and Adaptations

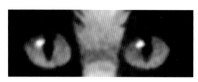

Cats have very large eyes for their body size to help them see in the dark. Like humans, the pupils open and close to let in more or less light as needed. Most non-roaring (small) cat pupils look more like tiny slits (to let only a little light in) when it is bright and big and round at night to let in lots of light.

Their eyes also act like mirrors at night to gather as much light as possible. That's why cat eyes glow or look red if caught in bright lights at night.

Like most predators, the eyes are on the front of the head (like our eyes) to judge distances. Cats can see more things in their "side" vision (peripheral) than we can.

Cats move each ear in different directions to track the sounds which helps them track their prey.

Unlike humans, cats can't taste much difference in foods.

Cat tongues are rough, like sandpaper, to help them drink water, to clean themselves, and to pull feathers, meat, and skin off the animals they eat.

Cats have a good sense of smell. Like many animals, cats "mark" their territory with smells. This tells other animals "stay out" or "this is mine." When a domestic cat rubs up against you, it is "marking you" to let other cats know that you belong to it. Cats and other animals also claw trees or go to the bathroom to mark territory.

Cats use their sense of touch as well as their eyes to help them move around in the dark. Their whiskers (vibrissae) sense changes in air currents to tell them where things are. When walking or pouncing on prey, cats' whiskers point forward to help them "see" in the dark. Blind pet cats can even walk around just using their whiskers to see! When sleeping or at rest, cats' whiskers are even with their heads.

Cats use their sharp claws to grab prey, fight, and climb trees. Most cats (except for cheetahs, fishing cats, and flat-headed cats) can pull (retract) their claws all the way inside their feet to help keep the claws nice and sharp. They sharpen claws on trees (or furniture).

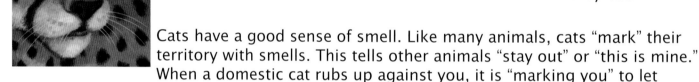

The soft pads on the bottom of cats' feet act like cushions. Some scientists think that cats sense vibrations through their pads, helping them to know when something moves.

All cats have long, sharp, knife-like teeth (canines) to stab and kill their prey. Other teeth are used to hold onto their prey and to tear the meat off the bones.

Cat True False Questions

Can you tell which statements are true and which are false? Answers are upside down, below.

1. Many wild cats are threatened or endangered because of loss of habitat or over hunting.

2. All wild cats live by themselves (solitary). Mother cats will send their kittens off to find their own territory as soon as they are grown.

3. Kittens have baby teeth that are replaced by adult teeth, just like us.

4. All cats are meat eaters. Wild cats must hunt for their food. Pet cats have instincts to hunt prey and will often kill birds or mice—even if they aren't hungry.

5. All cats grab prey with their paws.

6. All cats can eat while lying down.

7. Cheetahs prefer to chase their prey. Most other cats prefer to keep low to the ground to stalk their prey and will usually pounce quickly, but will chase prey if they have to.

8. Cats wag their tails only when happy.

9. All cats purr when happy.

10. Wild kittens will push their feet up and down (like kneading bread) on their mother while drinking milk. Pet cats will sometimes do this to the people in their lives.

11. Wild cats live on every continent except Australia and Antarctica.

12. Pet cats have some of the same behaviors as their wild cousins.

13. Cats have different colors of fur and patterns.

14. Cats can talk to each other and to other animals like they do in the story.

15. Some scientists think pet cats descended from wild cats in Africa.

Answers: 1. True—some cats have been hunted and killed just because people are afraid of them and other cats (tigers, snow leopards) have been killed for their fur or other body parts; 2. False—lions live in social groups (prides); 3. True; 4. True; 5. True; 6. True; 7. True; 8. False—a cat swishing its tail could mean that it is upset; 9. False—some cats roar, but cannot purr, and others can purr, but cannot roar; 10. True—maybe as a way of saying "you are mine."; 11. True; 12. True; 13. True; 14. False—many animals can communicate with each other but not by talking like we do; 15. True.

For Hudson, Isabella, Landon, and Nolan—SC

To the memory of my dear tortoiseshell, Phoebe—SD

The author is donating a portion of her royalties from this book to the Snow Leopard Trust.

Thanks to Craig Saffoe, Biologist and Curator (interim) Great Cats and Bears Exhibits at the Smithsonian National Zoological Park, for reviewing this book for accuracy.

Library of Congress Cataloging-in-Publication Data

Cohn, Scotti, 1950-
  Big cat, little kitty / by Scotti Cohn ; illustrated by Susan Detwiler.
    p. cm.
  ISBN 978-1-60718-124-8 (hardback) -- ISBN 978-1-60718-134-7 (pbk.)
-- ISBN 978-1-60718-144-6 (english ebook) -- ISBN 978-1-60718-154-5
(spanish ebook) 1. Wildcat--Juvenile literature. 2. Cats--Juvenile
literature. 3. Days--Juvenile literature. I. Detwiler, Susan, ill. II. Title.
  QL737.C23C636 2011
  599.75--dc22

                              2010049573

Also available as eBooks featuring auto-flip, auto-read, 3D-page-curling, and selectable English and Spanish text and audio
Interest level: 004-008
Grade level: P-3
ATOS™ Level: 2.6
Lexile Level: 500 Lexile Code: AD

Curriculum keywords: adaptations, anthropomorphic, antonyms/synonyms, compare/contrast, life science, map, repeating earth patterns, senses, threatened/endangered, time: days of week

Manufactured in China, January, 2011
This product conforms to CPSIA 2008
First Printing
Sylvan Dell Publishing
612 Johnnie Dodds Blvd., Suite A2
Mt. Pleasant, SC 29464